SLOTH'S SHOES

for my mother – J.W.
Amy and Kate, forever – T.R.

First American Edition 1998 by Kane/Miller Book Publishers
Brooklyn, New York & La Jolla, California

Originally published in Great Britain in 1997 by Andersen Press Ltd.

Text copyright © 1997 by Jeanne Willis
Illustrations copyright © 1997 by Tony Ross

Library of Congress Catalog Card Number 97-72908

ISBN 0-916291-78-2
Printed and bound in Italy by Grafiche AZ, Verona
1 2 3 4 5 6 7 8 9 10

Jeanne Willis and Tony Ross

SLOTH'S
SHOES

A CRANKY NELL BOOK

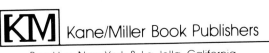

Kane/Miller Book Publishers

Brooklyn, New York & La Jolla, California

There was a tree that grew so high
It tickled the moon and stroked the sky,
It poked the sun and scratched the stars,
It played with Jupiter and Mars.

On top of the tree a small sloth swung.
He slept, he crept, he crawled, he clung,
Went one foot forward, two and then
He tiptoed three steps back again.

"Where are you going, I'd like to know?"
A Boomslang boomed from a branch below.
Three steps forward, three steps back,
Sloth clicked his claws with a clickety-clack.

"My birthday party starts at three,"
Quoth Sloth, "beneath this Thunder Tree.
You'll tell my friends? How kind of you!"
(Three steps forward. Backwards, two.)

Boomslang slip-slung down to Bird.
"Sloth's birthday party! Spread the word,"
He hissed. And Bird, with both wings spread,
Buttered and sliced some best brown bread.

"We'll bake the cake," barked the Baboons,
"We'll handle candles and balloons."
The Bees buzzed and the Potteroos
Stitched Sloth a pair of birthday shoes.

Such beautiful shoes with vine-twine ties
–His favourite shape! His perfect size!–
And lined with softest, moth-proof moss
And sewn with skeins of spiders' floss.

And all the while the plans were made
Sloth swung slowly in the shade.
Four steps forward he would creep,
Then three steps backwards, back to sleep.

"Peanuts!" proffered the Pangolin.
The Fruit Bat threw some berries in.
The Frog brought jelly, freshly laid,
While Jaguar jugged lemonade.

Down below the guest list grew—
The friends of Sloth were far from few.
But far from view was Sloth; the tree
Was very, very high, you see.

Time ticked by. It always does;
It never wants to wait for us.
It always likes to race us there
And then it's gone! But why? And where?

"It's five past three," said Jaguar,
"And as for Sloth, he can't be far.
So play the pipes and bang the drum
And sing and dance! He's bound to come."

The party went with such a swing
And yet the Sloth heard not a thing.
He slowed right up. He didn't care
To be the very first one there.

The sun went down, the moon was bright,
The party went on through the night;
Then through the day and through the week–
The creatures were too tired to speak.

Too tired, that is, except for Snake,
Who thought they ought to light the cake
Which had five candles on, I'm told,
Because the Sloth was five years old.

At least he was a while ago.
But oh, that Sloth was so, so slow
The weeks turned into months and then
Christmas came around again.

Two steps forward, three, then four–
Sloth just couldn't manage more.
He caught his breath and stood quite still,
And gasped that speed made sloths feel ill.

"This is silly!" bellowed Bat.
"Sloth's not coming. That is that!
Let's leave his birthday shoes and cake
And go to bed for goodness' sake."

And so they did that very night.
There were no animals in sight
Except for Sloth. For suddenly
He reached the bottom of the tree.

"That's odd," he thought, "there's no one here."
Poor Sloth! Right place, right day, wrong year.
His cake was short of candlesticks;
He took so long, there should be SIX.

A year had passed. They do, you know.
He'd grown so fast (and him so slow!)
It should be no surprise at all:
His birthday shoes were *far too small*.